Dear Parent:
Your child's love of reading starts here!

Every child learns to read in a different way and at his or her own speed. Some go back and forth between reading levels and read favorite books again and again. Others read through each level in order. You can help your young reader improve and become more confident by encouraging his or her own interests and abilities. From books your child reads with you to the first books he or she reads alone, there are I Can Read Books for every stage of reading:

SHARED READING
Basic language, word repetition, and whimsical illustrations, ideal for sharing with your emergent reader

BEGINNING READING
Short sentences, familiar words, and simple concepts for children eager to read on their own

READING WITH HELP
Engaging stories, longer sentences, and language play for developing readers

READING ALONE
Complex plots, challenging vocabulary, and high-interest topics for the independent reader

ADVANCED READING
Short paragraphs, chapters, and exciting themes for the perfect bridge to chapter books

I Can Read Books have introduced children to the joy of reading since 1957. Featuring award-winning authors and illustrators and a fabulous cast of beloved characters, I Can Read Books set the standard for beginning readers.

A lifetime of discovery begins with the magical words "I Can Read!"

Visit www.icanread.com for information
on enriching your child's reading experience.

I Can Read!™

READING
WITH HELP
2

FLAPPY
AND
SCRAPPY

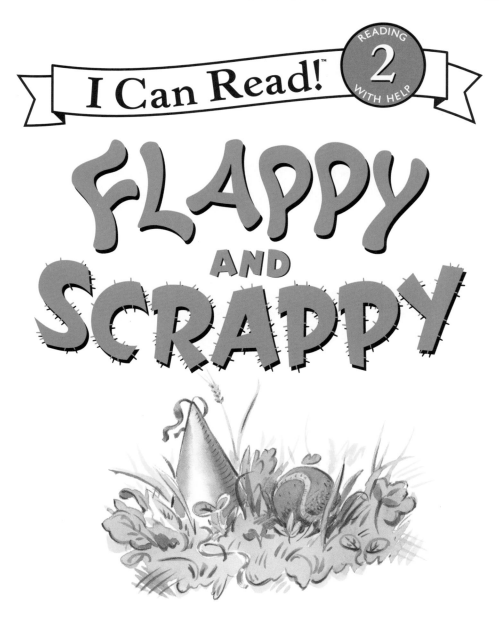

story by Arthur Yorinks
pictures by Aleksey and Olga Ivanov

HarperCollins*Publishers*

For all the border collies and poodles in heaven
and for this book's angel, Sally Doherty
—A.Y.

For N., A., and I.
—A. & O.I.

HarperCollins®, 🐾®, and I Can Read Book® are trademarks of HarperCollins Publishers.

Library of Congress Cataloging-in-Publication Data
Yorinks, Arthur.
    Flappy and Scrappy / by Arthur Yorinks ; [illustrations by Olga Ivanov]. — 1st ed.
       p.   cm. — (I can read book ; 2)
    Summary: After canine friends Scrappy and Flappy play an unusual game of catch, Scrappy complains that everyone has forgotten his birthday, but Flappy surprises him.
    ISBN 978-0-06-205117-2 (trade bdg.) ISBN 978-0-06-205913-0 (pbk.)
    [1. Dogs—Fiction.   2. Play—Fiction.   3. Surprise—Fiction.   4. Birthdays—Fiction.   5. Parties—Fiction.]   I. Ivanov, O. (Olga), ill.   II. Title.
PZ7.Y819Ff   2011   2008027467
[E]—dc22   CIP
AC

11 12 13 14 15   SCP   10 9 8 7 6 5 4 3 2 1   ❖   First Edition

Contents

Good Friends

It was a nice spring day.

"I will visit my friend Scrappy,"

said Flappy.

So she walked up Sheep's Hill.

"Hello, Sheep," said Flappy.

Sheep tried to say "Hello, Flappy,"

but she was eating grass.

It sounded like "Hi-ho, Fatty!"

8

"Well, hello Fatty to you!"
said Flappy.

Then Flappy walked down the hill

to a field filled with cows.

"Hello, cows," said Flappy.

The cows were eating, too.

"Moo-moo, Frumpy,"

they said with their mouths full.

"Frumpy!" said Flappy.

"I just got brushed!"

Flappy walked through the field

to the pigpen.

"Hi, Pig," she said.

"I'm going to Scrappy's house."

Pig was loving his lunch.

"Ga-ga, Grumpy!" he squealed.

Flappy turned and growled.

"If you can't say something nice,"

she said, "don't say anything!"

Flappy came to a big oak tree.

"This is a nice spot to rest,"

she said.

Flappy heard "Chirp, chirp!"

She looked up and saw a bird.

"Hello, Bird. What a sunny day,"

said Flappy.

Bird was eating a tasty worm.

She spoke with her mouth full.

It sounded like, "Ya-ya, go away!"

Flappy was sad.

"Maybe nobody likes me," she cried.

She walked past the horses

and past the goats

and past the chickens

and she didn't say a word.

She walked with her head down
all the way to Scrappy's house.
Scrappy was sitting on his porch.
He had a biscuit in his mouth.
"Hello, Scrappy," said Flappy softly.

Scrappy put his biscuit down.

"Hello, Flappy!" he said.

Flappy kissed Scrappy on the nose.

Then she barked and said,

"Scrappy, you are my best friend!"

Play Ball

One day, Flappy went to Scrappy.

Flappy had a rubber ball.

"What are you doing with that ball?"
asked Scrappy.

"I want to play catch," said Flappy.

"Oh," said Scrappy. "What is catch?"

"You push the ball with your nose,"
said Flappy, "and then I catch it."

"I'm not playing," said Scrappy.

"It's fun," said Flappy.

"I'd rather eat grass," said Scrappy.

"Me, too," said Sheep.

"I love eating grass."

"Sheep, will you play catch with me?"
asked Flappy.

"No," said Sheep.

"No one will play with me,"
said Flappy.

She was very sad.

"Oh, all right," said Scrappy.

"I'll play."

"Me, too," said Sheep.

Sheep tried to play first.

She put her nose to the ground.

She smelled the grass.

It smelled so good,

she forgot about the ball.

She started eating the grass.

"That's not how to play," said Flappy.

Cow stopped by to say hello.

"Will you play catch with me?"

asked Flappy.

"Sure," said Cow. "How do you play?"

"Just push the ball with your nose,"

said Flappy, "and I'll catch it!"

Cow lowered her nose to the ground

and smelled the grass.

"Don't eat the grass!" yelled Flappy.

But it was too late.

Cow munched and munched.

"Oh, please don't eat the grass!"

said Flappy.

"What's the matter?" asked Pig.

"No one will play catch with me," said Flappy.

"I'll play," said Pig.

"You will?" asked Flappy.

"Sure!" said Pig.

"And you won't eat the grass?"

"Of course not," said Pig.

Flappy was happy.

She moved back

to get ready to catch the ball.

Pig walked up to the ball
and scratched at the grass
in front of it.

"Now, push it with your nose,"

Flappy called out.

Pig lowered his nose.

"Give the ball a good push!"

Flappy shouted.

But Pig did not push the ball.

He started eating the dirt.

"I love dirt!" said Pig.

Flappy was not happy.

She started to run.

She ran very fast toward the ball.

She pushed the ball so hard
it went flying into the air.
Scrappy looked up.
He opened his mouth
and caught the ball!

"You caught it! You caught it!"

cried Flappy.

"We played catch!"

"I'd still rather eat grass,"

said Scrappy,

"but it was a good throw, Flappy."

"Good catch, Scrappy," said Flappy.

A Birthday

Flappy and Scrappy went for a walk.

Flappy looked at Scrappy.

"Why are you sad?" asked Flappy.

"It's my birthday today," said Scrappy,

"and no one said happy birthday to me."

"Not Sheep?" asked Flappy.

"No," said Scrappy.

"Not Cow?" asked Flappy.

"No," said Scrappy.

"Not Pig?" asked Flappy.

"Not Pig or even Horse!"
said Scrappy.

"I did not say happy birthday
to you, either," said Flappy.

"No, you did not," said Scrappy.

"I'm sorry," said Flappy.

"That's all right," said Scrappy.

But it was not all right.

Scrappy looked like
he was going to cry.

"I know what to do," said Flappy.

"Let's visit Sheep.

She will say happy birthday to you."

Flappy and Scrappy walked

to Sheep's Hill.

"Sheep is not here," said Scrappy.

37

"Let's go see Cow," said Flappy.

"She will moo happy birthday to you."

Flappy and Scrappy walked

to the field,

but there was not one cow to be seen.

"Where is she?" asked Flappy.

"No one will say happy birthday
to me," said Scrappy.
"Pig must be home," said Flappy.
"Let's go visit him."
Flappy and Scrappy walked
to Pig's pen.
But Pig was not there.

"Maybe they are saying happy birthday

to someone else," said Scrappy.

"Just not me."

"I am sure Horse is home,"

said Flappy.

"Let's go to the barn.

I will race you!"

Flappy and Scrappy raced to the barn.

It was empty.

"I am sorry no one is home,"

said Flappy.

"Thank you for trying,"

said Scrappy.

Scrappy was very sad.

"You can come to my house,"

said Flappy.

"We can dig a hole

or chew on something."

"I will just go home," said Scrappy.

"Please," said Flappy.

"Come to my house."

"All right," said Scrappy.

"Just for a minute."

Flappy and Scrappy walked

along the stream and over the hill

to Flappy's house.

"What's that sound?" asked Scrappy.

There was a lot of noise

in Flappy's house.

"Let's see," said Flappy.

Flappy opened the door.

There was Sheep. And Cow.

And Pig. And Horse.

And when they saw Scrappy,

they all shouted,

"Happy birthday, Scrappy!"

Flappy looked at her friend
and said, "Happy birthday, Scrappy."
Scrappy had a very happy birthday.